THE GREAT

For Nancy and Mike,
all the way over in Green Bay.
Miss yooz lots Nanc!
CF

To Mum and Dad
KH

SIMON AND SCHUSTER
First published in Great Britain in 2012
by Simon and Schuster UK Ltd
1st Floor, 222 Gray's Inn Road, London WC1X 8HB
A CBS Company

978-0-85707-262-7 (HB)
978-0-85707-263-4 (PB)
978-0-85707-708-0 (eBook)

Printed in China
10 9 8 7 6 5 4 3 2 1

THE GREAT ...RTLE ...NT

SNORTLE HUNT

Claire Freedman

Illustrated by
Kate Hindley

SIMON AND SCHUSTER
London New York Sydney Toronto New Delhi

On a hill bumpy-steepy,
  there's a house **scary-creepy**,

And it's said that a **Snortle** lives there.

Now **nobody's** been,

so **nobody's** seen,

But Mouse whispers, "Come, if you **dare!**"

As soon as it's **dark**, they meet in the park,

Mouse says,
"Snortles **love** moonlit nights."

Between them they take,
a torch,
rope and
cake,

TRACKS TRAILS

For Snortles have huge appetites!

It's scarily still, as they creep up the hill,

Mouse whispers,

"Sshh, Cat – no more talking."

"Don't tell me to hush - it's from behind us,
Do you think that the Snortle's out walking?"

"That's silly!" says Mouse, "he'll be holed in his house,
There's no one, but me and you two."

"I'm s-s-ure s-s-**something's** here,"
Dog stutters in fear,

Then, suddenly, someone calls,
"**WOOOOOOO!**"

The three of them **jump**!

Cat **drops** her torch,

thump!

As Rabbit leaps out from the trees,

"Phew! Rabbit it's you –
and not You Know Who!"

Says Rabbit, "Can I join you,
please?"

The wind whistles

-eek!

Tall tree branches creak,

They lift up the latch to the gate.

Dog gulps. "If we wake him, all angry we'll make him."
Mouse laughs, "Snortles go to bed late."

The door's open wide,
so they all creep inside,

Cat warns, "**Wait!** This could be a trap!"

"Let's scarper!" they cry,
but there's no time to try,

As the door bangs shut-tight with a **SNAP!**

The torch splutters, PHOOT!

Now it's blacker than soot,

Dog squeaks, "We have nowhere to flee!"

Mouse whispers, "Look,

there's a dim light up the stairs,

And now that we're here we must see!"

They climb to the top,
then come to a stop,
They're dreading just what they might find,

For the growls
and the groans,
and strange gurgly moans,
Are the horribly Snortley kind!

Their hearts beat **boom, boom,**
as they creep in the room,

On the bed sleeps a **monster-huge** shape.

Cat gasps. "He's **enormous!** He's stirring!
He SAW us! Before he wakes up let's escape!"

They scramble outside,
down the drainpipe they slide,
It swings with a shuddering shake!
The drainpipe's too old,
it's not going to hold,
and the Snortle is now **wide awake!**

"He's coming!" they shout,
as a hand reaches out!
All hairy with horrible claws.

His eyes have a **gleam,**

like nothing they've seen,

"WHAT ARE YOU ALL DOING?"

he roars.

The Snortle's so near, they're frozen with fear,
Cat quivers and Mouse gives a yelp!

"Oi!"
he growls . . .

The very next day, the Snortle (hooray!)
Invites them all over for tea.

Says Mouse, "Snortles tend to make super friends."
And for once they all laugh and agree!